HANNAH AND THE HOMUNCULUS

For Ami & Ruta—each a feisty, female character in her own right.
Kurt Hassler

For John & Jean, my Dad & Mom. Thanks!
K.L Darnell

Text copyright © 2001 Sleeping Bear Press
Illustrations copyright © 2001 Kathryn Darnell

Sleeping Bear Press
310 North Main Street
P.O. Box 20
Chelsea, MI 48118
www.sleepingbearpress.com

Printed and bound in Canada.

10 9 8 7 6 5 4 3 2 1

Library of Congress Cataloging-in-Publication Data on File
ISBN: 1-58536-043-0

Hannah
AND THE HOMUNCULUS

By Kurt Hassler

Illustrated By Kathryn Darnell

Sleeping Bear Press

The smell woke Hannah. Still sleepy, she scrunched her face, but the smoky scent of musky grass clippings made the young girl's eyes water. It was then that Hannah felt something slither between her bare toes.

It felt like a shoelace, but it tickled something awful. Hannah's first thought might have been *What is it?* but instinct took control. The young girl leapt from her bed, scattering the covers. Before she even realized, the word burst from her lips.

Hannah wasn't one to keep her feelings to herself. She might've woken the whole neighborhood with that explosive: "No!"

But Hannah didn't wake the
neighborhood. No sooner had the
word slipped her tongue than a ratty
rag doll sprung from her bed, catching
that "**NO**" in a jar. Now this wasn't one of
Hannah's dolls. She'd shaved the hair off all her
dolls years ago. The doll bursting from Hannah's
bedsheets had button eyes and a mop of dusty,
matted, yarn hair. It struck Hannah as a curious
character—mostly because it was alive. The nimble doll
fastened the lid on the jar and then scurried out the door
like a rodent.

Thinking the whole thing a dream, Hannah climbed back into
bed and straightened the covers, giving no more thought to her
strange visitor. By morning, she'd all but forgotten him.

More's the pity for her...

When Hannah sat down to breakfast the next day, her father asked, "Would you like some oatmeal, Hannah?" Now Hannah's father asked this every morning, knowing full well that Hannah hated oatmeal. Hannah didn't think it very funny and knew her reply by rote. Crossing her arms and tilting her head (as if to say, "Dad, you are *so* not funny"), Hannah in her most confident manner said...

Absolutely nothing.

Where was her **NO?** She'd had it yesterday. Why, she must have used it a hundred times! "No, I don't like that dress on you, Mom," she'd said, and "No, Mrs. Farrah, I don't have my homework." She certainly remembered saying, "No, I don't want any oatmeal, Dad." So where was her **NO** today? Flabbergasted, her mouth hung open so wide she looked like a flounder. Delighted, her father plopped a heaping bowl of oatmeal in front of her. He'd never seen his daughter so easily swayed!

Hannah was angrily kicking a can around the driveway, trying to forget the taste of oatmeal, when her mother caught up with her.

"Hannah, how about cleaning the garage for me this morning?"

She used a voice that was much too sweet. Hannah's father must have reported how agreeable Hannah had been at the breakfast table. This made the young girl fume so that saying no should have been a snap. Sure it would be! Hannah screwed up her face and tried. She tried so hard that her face turned bright red, then blue, and finally magenta. She tried so hard her toes curled and her eyes rolled. And...

Not a thing.

Dizzy and out of breath, Hannah let her mother lead her off to the garage where she spent the rest of the morning sweeping and hauling paint cans. She was too exhausted to raise a fuss.

Hannah soon realized things were getting serious. In one morning she'd pleased her father and her mother. Imagine! What if she never got her **NO** back? It was too horrible to think about. Then in the back of her head Hannah remembered her dream, but didn't have time to think about it too much.

"Hannah, dear? Hannah!"

The sound of her grandmother's voice made Hannah say something that she would have been grounded for had anyone overheard her. Afraid to wait for another word and get stuck pulling weeds or washing the car, Hannah charged into the woods behind her house. Let anyone find her there!

Back in the woods, Hannah spent the afternoon puzzling over her situation. Recalling the rag doll from her dream, she grew convinced that it had something to do with the disappearance of her **NO**. But how could she find that doll? The woods were getting dark and her stomach was growling. Soon she'd have to go back, but without her **NO**, she'd be at the adults' terrible mercy. Hannah sat down on a rock, depressed, when her face clenched up at a smoky scent she recognized right away!

Tracing a tiny wisp of smoke back to its source, Hannah found a tall, rotten, old, tree stump. Getting on her hands and knees, she peered through a small slot. Inside the stump, in a tidy little study sat the rag doll before his fireplace. Stoked with twigs and musky grass clippings, the smell, which clung to the rag doll, made Hannah's eyes water worse than the night before. Not so much, though, that she couldn't see the rows and rows of glass jars lining the study walls like so many little books. Each jar had a word printed on it, and on a velvet cushion on the mantelpiece sat a special jar stenciled with the word: **NO**.
It was Hannah's **NO**! She knew it! Muttering to herself, she squeezed a hand through an opening in the stump and grabbed that jar, lickety-split!

"Intruder!" squeaked the rag doll, jumping up and poking his stick at her. "Thief!" he cried furiously, but Hannah paid him no mind. Who was he to talk?

When she tried to free her clenched hand from the stump, though, Hannah found her fist too big for the tiny opening. To free her hand, she'd have to let go of the jar that contained her **NO**, but she wasn't about to do that!

"Rascal!" jeered the doll inside, delighted by Hannah's predicament. "Thwarted!" he said triumphantly, thinking himself the victor, but Hannah set him straight.

"As long as I'm stuck, then you're stuck!"
she called.

Looking around, the rag doll quickly saw the truth in this. The stump had only one exit, and Hannah's fist had it clogged. "Impasse," sighed the doll, sinking into his armchair. "Stalemate."

Hannah thought she had him.

"Are you going to give me back what you took, then?"

The rag doll leapt to his feet. "No!" he shouted using Hannah's own NO against her. He knew well the power of words, you see. A word had given him life. Homunculus! That was the word that sparked life in him one day when his owner said it aloud. Homunculus! He snatched hold of that word and scampered off with it. Ever since, that was what he called himself. Oh, every word had power, the Homunculus knew, and like Hannah, he wasn't about to give up the formidable "NO."

So there the two of them stewed, stubborn and unbending. Only when her knees began to ache and her back grew stiff did Hannah suppose there might be a better way.

"What if I told you," she suggested, "that if you gave back this word that I could get you another exactly like it? You wouldn't have to lift a finger." The Homunculus was tempted. Hannah could tell, so she sweetened the pot. "I'll even throw a nice 'STOP' into the bargain. What do you think?"

Hungry to build his vocabulary, the Homunculus couldn't resist.

"Compromise?" he inquired, then demanded eagerly: "Explain…"

The next morning, after Hannah and the Homunculus completed their transaction, she skipped merrily down to the breakfast table.

"Oatmeal for breakfast today?" her father asked as usual.

"**No,**" Hannah pronounced expertly. (She was looking forward to breaking that word back in!) "I think I'll just have ice cream and some leftover cake. That is okay with you, isn't it?" she asked, snickering quietly.

Hannah watched her father's face turn bright red, then blue, and finally magenta. He couldn't understand it.

Sometime during the night, he seemed to have lost his **NO**.